new batch

Emily's Cupcake Magic!

By Coco Simon
author of Cupcake Diaries

Illustrated by Manuela López

Simon Spotlight
New York London Toronto Sydney New Delhi

This book is a work of fiction. Any references to historical events, real people, or real places are used fictitiously. Other names, characters, places, and events are products of the author's imagination, and any resemblance to actual events or places or persons, living or dead, is entirely coincidental.

SIMON SPOTLIGHT

An imprint of Simon & Schuster Children's Publishing Division

1230 Avenue of the Americas, New York, New York 10020

This Simon Spotlight edition May 2024

Copyright © 2024 by Simon & Schuster, LLC

All rights reserved, including the right of reproduction in whole or in part in any form.

SIMON SPOTLIGHT and colophon are registered trademarks of Simon & Schuster, LLC.

Simon & Schuster: Celebrating 100 Years of Publishing in 2024

For information about special discounts for bulk purchases, please contact Simon & Schuster Special Sales at 1-866-506-1949 or business@simonandschuster.com.

Text by Tracey West

Designed by Brittany Fetcho

Illustrations by Manuela López

The illustrations for this book were rendered digitally.

The text of this book was set in Bembo Std.

Manufactured in the United States of America 0324 OFF

2 4 6 8 10 9 7 5 3 1

Library of Congress Cataloging-in-Publication Data

Names: Simon, Coco, author. | López, Manuela, 1985– illustrator.

Title: Emily's cupcake magic! / by Coco Simon ; illustrated by Manuela López.

ription: Simon Spotlight edition. | New York : Simon Spotlight, 2024. | Series:
ke diaries: the new batch | Audience: Ages 5 to 9. | Summary: Cupcake Club
Katie Brown's stepsister Emily enters a baking contest at her new school and
discovers her own way to bake.

tifiers: LCCN 2023030122 (print) | LCCN 2023030123 (ebook)
9781665949101 (paperback) | ISBN 9781665949118 (hardcover)
ISBN 9781665949125 (ebook)

ndship—Fiction. | Contests—Fiction. | Baking—Fiction. | Schools—Fiction.
Family life—Fiction. | BISAC: JUVENILE FICTION / Social Themes /
ndship | JUVENILE FICTION / Cooking & Food
0357 Ee 2024 (print) | LCC PZ7.S60357 (ebook) | DDC [Fic]—dc23
available at https://lccn.loc.gov/2023030122
rd available at https://lccn.loc.gov/2023030123

CONTENTS

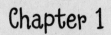

Chapter 1

What Friends?

Beep beep boop! Beep beep boop!

Ugh! That sound meant it was time to wake up. I opened my eyes. I tried to focus on the color of my bedroom walls. . . .

My name is Emily Green. My parents are divorced. Sometimes I sleep at my mom's house. And sometimes I sleep at my dad's house. I'm still getting used to my dad's new house. There's a lot to get used to here. Besides being in a new place, I have to get used to spending time with my new stepsister, Katie, and my stepmom, Sharon. And when I'm sleepy, sometimes I forget which house I'm in.

My bedroom walls are pink. That means I'm at Dad and Sharon's house. My bedroom walls at Mom's house are yellow. So yesterday was a Dad day.

I got ready for school. Downstairs in the kitchen, Dad was filling his coffee mug. Sharon had already left to go to work. Katie was packing our lunch bags.

"Turkey and Swiss okay, Em?" she asked. "We're out of tuna."

"That's great," I said. "Thanks, Katie."

Then Katie held up two cupcakes.
Each was in its own plastic container.

"One for you. And one for a friend,"
she said. "The Cupcake Club made a
test batch last night. They're cookies-
and-cream flavored."

I wanted to say, *But I don't have any friends. Not anymore.*

But I didn't. Instead, I said, "Sounds yummy."

Then I poured myself some cereal. I stared into the bowl, feeling sad. A week ago, my entire life had changed. It all felt really scary.

I used to go to Hamilton Elementary School. Then the whole plumbing system busted. The first floor got flooded. Now everyone has to go to different schools until Hamilton gets fixed. Some went to Fenton Street School. The rest went to Sunrise Hill Elementary.

I got sent to Fenton Street. And all my friends got sent to Sunrise Hill. Abby. Ivy. Ryan. Samantha. *All* of them! It was so unfair!

My first week at Fenton had been awful. I had to get used to a new building. New teachers. It was very confusing.

I missed my friends. And I hadn't made any new ones yet. I'm pretty shy.

I'll probably never have friends again, I thought.

"Gotta run!" Dad said, kissing the top of my head. "Katie, please see that Emily gets to her bus stop."

"When have I ever failed you, Jeff?" she asked. Then she looked at me, smiled, winked, and gave me a big hug.

Dad left. Katie looked at me again.

"You okay, Em? Your cereal is getting soggy."

"I—it's just hard going to a new school," I said.

Katie nodded. "Yeah, when I started middle school, it was really hard."

"What made it better?" I asked.

"Honestly? Cupcakes!" Katie replied. She put my lunch bag down in front of me. "I'll tell you the whole story sometime. For now, just trust in cupcake magic!" She wiggled her fingers in a silly way.

I knew Katie was just trying to make me feel better. But part of me hoped the cupcakes really *were* magic. I needed *something* to help me get through another day at Fenton Street School!

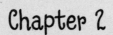

Chapter 2

Cupcake Magic

I climbed on the school bus and hurried toward some empty seats in the back.

"Hey, Emily! Over here!"

I stopped. A girl with wavy brown hair was calling me over. It was Natalie Ruiz, from my softball team. I slid into the seat next to her.

"Hi," I said.

"I thought I saw you in my math class," she said. "But this is the first time

I've seen you on the school bus."

I blushed a little. Sometimes it's hard to explain that I live in two different places. "I take a different bus when I stay at my mom's."

Natalie nodded. "Yeah, my friend Alana does that too. Do you know her? Alana Wilson?"

Of course I knew Alana! I remembered her as one of the popular girls back at Hamilton. Natalie was pretty popular too.

Natalie's being nice, I thought. *But she probably doesn't want to be friends with somebody shy like me.*

"I had gym with Alana," I said.

"Can you believe she's my only friend who got sent to Fenton? Everyone else I know ended up at Sunrise Hill!" Natalie complained.

"Me too," I said. "This whole thing is so unfair."

"Totally!" Natalie agreed. "Hey, you should sit with me and Alana at lunch today. We Hamilton kids have to stick together!"

"Yeah!" I agreed. I was so excited! "Lunch. For sure. Definitely!"

Natalie and I talked the rest of the way to school. She was easy to talk to. We didn't know each other well, but I didn't feel like I had to search for things to talk about with her. After that, I was in a good mood all morning. I had someone to eat lunch with!

When lunchtime finally came, I found Natalie and Alana at a table by themselves. With her braided black hair and cute denim jacket, Alana looked super stylish.

"Alana, this is Emily. From Hamilton, remember?" Natalie asked.

"Hi, Emily!" Alana said cheerfully. "Natalie and I were talking about that guy on YouChannel who eats all those hot peppers. Isn't he hilarious?"

"Um," I replied. I'd never watched him. Alana and Natalie kept talking and laughing.

Come on, Emily. Think of something to say! I told myself. I started feeling left out.

I opened my lunch bag and saw the two cupcakes Katie had packed.

"I brought cupcakes!" I blurted out. "They're cookies-and-cream flavored. My stepsister, Katie, is in the Cupcake Club and—"

Alana turned to me. "The Cupcake Club? Really? I saw them on the news once. Their cupcakes are supposed to be so good. Can we really try them?"

"Sure," I said, handing one each to Natalie and Alana.

"We can cut them in half so you can have some," Natalie offered.

"That's okay," I said. "I eat cupcakes all the time at home. I help Katie bake sometimes too."

"Lucky!" Alana said. "I love to bake."

"Me too. Especially cupcakes," Natalie added.

They both ate their cupcakes. We talked about cupcakes, our new teachers, and our friends back at Hamilton.

I couldn't believe it. I'd started the morning with no friends at school. And now I had two!

I have to remember to tell Katie that the cupcake magic worked! I thought.

Chapter 3

Let's Bake!

The next day, the cupcake magic continued. Principal Estrella made a special announcement in the morning over the loudspeaker.

"Students, I first want to say that everyone is doing a great job of working together these last few days," she began. "There have been a lot of changes for everyone, but we're getting through it with flying colors."

Lots of kids clapped and cheered.

"To celebrate, we're going to hold a special baking contest," Principal Estrella went on. "Two weeks from today, after school. It's a great way to make new friends. Everyone who wants to can participate. We want you to work in teams of four. Bake up something special for the contest. The teachers will judge. We're sending home a flyer with the details."

Everyone began to talk and whisper at once. All I kept thinking was: *If I could win a baking contest, everyone would know me. Everyone would like me. I'd be one of the cool kids! I'd be popular!*

At lunchtime, I couldn't wait to talk to Natalie and Alana.

"Can you believe it?" I asked. "A baking contest. It's perfect for us!"

"Definitely!" Alana agreed.

Natalie frowned. "Except, there are only three of us and we need a group of four."

Alana looked around the cafeteria. She
pointed to a girl sitting by herself, reading
a book. Her long black hair had a blue and
purple streak in it. "What about her? Ren
Lu. She's in my English class. I think she's
new. Like, not from Fenton or Hamilton."

"I've met her," Natalie said. "She's
nice."

"You mean just walk over and talk to her?" I asked nervously.

Alana stood up. "Sure," she said.

Alana approached Ren. They talked for a few seconds. Then Ren closed her book. They both came to our table.

"This is Natalie, and this is Emily," Alana said, pointing.

Ren slid into a seat. "Hi," she said shyly. She was blushing a little. "Thanks for letting me . . . I mean. I don't know anybody yet. This is nice."

Alana sat down. "Can we meet at my house tomorrow? We can talk about what we want to bake for the contest."

"Maybe we could do a practice bake," I suggested. "Katie and her friends in the Cupcake Club do that all the time."

Alana bit her lip. "We'll *never* be as good as the Cupcake Club, will we?"

Ren piped up softly. "You never know until you try. That's what my grandmother always says, anyway."

"We are going to be awesome," Natalie said confidently.

For the rest of the day, I couldn't stop thinking about the baking contest. As soon as I got to Mom's house, my team and I texted one another ideas on our tablets.

In the middle of all this, I got a group text from Abby and Ivy, my best friends from Hamilton.

Abby: We miss you!

Ivy: School is not the same without you. Is it horrible at Fenton?

Emily: It's OK. I miss you too.

I did miss them—that was true. But for the first time, I felt like I might actually *like* being at Fenton!

Chapter 4

The worst
cupcakes ever?

The next day after school, we met at Alana's house. Her mom was home, and her two younger brothers were running around. The kitchen was all set up for us.

"The oven is preheating right now," Mrs. Wilson said. "I'll keep the boys out of here while you're baking. Just remember, Alana, to call me before touching the oven. And clean up after yourselves."

"Yes, Mom," Alana promised. She

looked at me. "Okay, Emily, how do you want to start?"

"Me?" I asked.

"You've baked with the Cupcake Club," Alana said. "We should do it like they do."

I thought quickly. I *had* baked with them before.

"First, we make the cupcake batter," I said. "While the cupcakes are baking, we make the frosting and get the decorations ready."

Ren held out a piece of paper. "I printed out the recipe we decided on. Mini chocolate cupcakes—"

"With salted caramel frosting!" Natalie finished for her. "My *abuela* has a yummy recipe. It's my favorite."

"Let the cupcake magic begin!" I cheered.

But our baking session was not very magical.

When we were making the batter, Alana added *a lot* of cinnamon. "To make it interesting," she said.

She also put rose water in the frosting. "To make it *more* interesting."

Then we almost burned the cupcakes. Natalie was supposed to be watching the time. "I went to set the timer, but then I wanted to see Alana make the frosting and I forgot," she said.

Ren volunteered to be in charge of decorations. We wanted a cute little red heart on top of each cupcake. Ren used kitchen scissors to cut out the tiny hearts from fruit strips. Then she used tweezers to place each one on top.

"They have to be perfect," she said.

It took forever!

Finally, the cupcakes were finished. They looked adorable. But then we tasted them. The bottoms were burnt. The cinnamon was very spicy. And the rose water added to the frosting made it taste weird.

I didn't want to say anything, but Natalie spoke up right away.

"These are *awful!*" she said.

"Yeah," Alana agreed sadly. "I guess they're *too* interesting."

Ren shook her head. "Let's face it. We have no chance of winning this contest. We're not like the Cupcake Club."

Then I had an idea. A really good idea.

"Don't worry," I said. "I know what we can do."

Chapter 5

Perfectly Sweet

I kept my idea a secret from Natalie, Alana, and Ren. I invited them over for another baking session, when I knew it was going to be a Dad day.

They were all very curious when they walked into my kitchen.

"So, what's the surprise, Emily?" Ren asked.

I smiled. I'm good at keeping secrets!

"You'll know in a little bit," I said.

"First, let's make another batch of those mini cupcakes."

Natalie threw up her hands. "Just don't ask me to time them!"

I held up a little windup kitchen timer shaped like a chicken. "It's okay. We can use this one."

We got to work. Alana still wanted to put cinnamon in the cake batter, but not so much this time. And she put almond extract in the frosting instead of rose water.

We didn't burn the mini cupcakes. And I helped Ren with the tiny hearts. It still took kind of a long time. In fact, we were still cutting out the hearts when my surprise arrived.

"We're here!"

Katie walked into the kitchen, followed by the rest of her friends in the Cupcake Club. Glamorous Mia, with her long, dark hair. Friendly Emma, with blond hair and blue eyes. And super-smart Alexis, with her wavy red hair.

The look on Natalie's face was priceless. "The Cupcake Club?!"

"You're all so cute," Katie said. "It's like you're the Mini Cupcake Club!"

"And they even made mini cupcakes!" Mia said, pointing. "And Emily is like a mini you. I wonder who the mini Mia is?" We all laughed.

I'm a mini Katie? I wasn't sure how I felt about that. I mean, I'm glad she's my big sister. But we are not the same. Katie is messy, and I'm neat. Katie loves running, and I think it's boring.

I didn't have time to think about what Mia said. I had to introduce everybody. "Katie and her friends said they would give us some pointers. To help us win the contest."

Alana grinned. "Like a secret weapon!"

"We can't bake for you. We're just here to give you our advice," Alexis said seriously.

"Yes, and eat cupcakes," Emma added. "Minis are my favorite!"

Ren held up the plate of cupcakes we had finished so far. Katie and her friends each took one. My new friends and I watched quietly as they ate.

"Well . . . ," Katie began.

"Tell us the truth. We can take it," Alana said.

Alexis spoke up. "The almond in the frosting is a little too much."

"But the cinnamon is a nice touch in the cake," Emma added.

Katie nodded. "Yeah. It's fun to experiment with flavors. But it's best to keep things simple, especially when you're starting out. People like basic flavors best, anyway, like vanilla and chocolate."

Mia chimed in. "The little fruit strip heart is cute," she said. Then she nodded toward the scissors on the table. "It's probably taking you a long time to cut each one out. Katie, you have mini shape cutters, right?"

"In the pantry," Katie replied.

A few minutes later, Mia was showing us how to use these tiny metal stamps to punch out the shapes in the fruit leather.

"This is definitely much faster! Thanks, Mia!" Ren said happily. And there were so many cute shapes to pick from too!

"This will help you make sure all your cupcakes look the same," Mia told us.

"So, to sum up, stick with the salted caramel frosting, but no almond, and use the shape cutter to speed things up. Then you should have a winner on your hands," Alexis said.

"Yeah, you're doing a great job," Katie said. "And I'm sure you'll do a great job cleaning up after yourselves as well. It's our turn to bake next."

"Just give us a few minutes," I said.

Katie and her friends left the kitchen. As they were going upstairs, I heard Emma say, "Katie, your little sister is so cute!"

"I know. I'm really proud of her," Katie replied.

Okay, I still didn't want to be a miniature version of Katie. But knowing that she was proud of me felt really sweet!

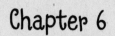

Chapter 6

The Contest

"There's the cupcake table!" Natalie said, pointing.

The school cafeteria was decorated with balloons and streamers for the baking contest. Tables were set up for everyone to display their entries.

We walked past the tables topped with cookies, cakes, pies, brownies, and muffins. When we got to the cupcake table, we all admired our mini cupcakes.

"They look so pretty," I said.

"What's our competition?" Alana wondered. She paced up and down the table. "Banana cupcakes. Birthday party cupcakes. *Pizza* cupcakes?"

A girl behind us heard Alana. "Ethan Moore's team baked those pizza cupcakes. They're going to win—it's such a cool idea. I wish I'd thought of it!"

"Ethan? Who's he?" Natalie wanted to know, but the girl walked away.

Principal Estrella stood in the middle of the room, holding a microphone. "All right, everybody, step away from the tables," she said. "The judges are going to start tasting your entries. When they're done, everyone will get to try these delicious baked goods."

We all stepped back to watch. Two teachers judged each table. Principal Estrella was one of the judges at the cupcake table.

I heard a boy's voice behind me. "She's trying a pizza cupcake!"

I turned and saw a boy with dark brown curly hair. *That must be Ethan,* I thought.

"How are we going to beat pizza cupcakes?" I whispered to Natalie. "That's so creative."

"Yeah, but remember what Katie said," Natalie whispered back. "People like basic flavors best. And we did chocolate cupcakes with salted caramel frosting, which is creative *and* playing it safe. So it's like we did both!"

After what seemed like forever, Principal Estrella announced that the judging was over. Everybody ran to their respective tables. My heart was beating fast.

Each plate of cupcakes had a paper star in front of it.

The banana cupcakes' star read: BEST USE OF FRUIT.

The birthday party cupcakes' star read: MOST COLORFUL.

The pizza cupcakes' star read: MOST CREATIVE.

And the star by our cupcakes read: BEST OVERALL CUPCAKES.

"We got best overall!" Alana yelled.

"That means our cupcakes were not only delicious, but they looked beautiful too!" Ren said. And we all started hugging and jumping up and down.

BEST
OVERALL
CUPCAKES

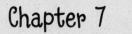

Chapter 7

A Mini Cupcake Club?

Principal Estrella walked up to us.

"Girls, your cupcakes were so delicious," she said. "I loved the small size. And they looked so yummy too. I've heard that some of the best chefs in the world say you eat with your eyes first."

We all thanked her.

"Where did you get your inspiration?" she asked.

"We made chocolate cupcakes

because, well, most people like chocolate," Natalie explained. "But we made the frosting from a recipe of my *abuela*'s. She's famous for her signature frosting flavors!" Natalie's eyes sparkled with pride as she spoke.

Then Alana piped up. "Emily's big sister, Katie, is in the Cupcake Club," she said. "They gave us some tips."

She didn't mean anything by it, but it bugged me a little that Alana implied that the Cupcake Club was our inspiration. That wasn't exactly true. We all worked together to come up with our recipe. And our decorations. Katie had nothing to do with it.

Principal Estrella smiled. "Ah, yes, the Cupcake Club. I had some of their cupcakes at my niece's baby shower. Say, wouldn't it be wonderful if Fenton Street School had its very own Cupcake Club?"

"That's a great idea!" Alana said. "You mean, it could be an official school club?"

"I don't see why not," the principal replied. "Think about it, girls."

She walked away. Alana, Natalie, and Ren started squealing with delight.

"We should do it!" Alana said.

"It could be the *Mini* Cupcake Club, like Mia called it," Ren said.

I didn't say anything. I saw Ren look at me. Did she know what I was thinking?

I wasn't sure I wanted to be in a copycat club. I didn't want to be a mini Katie.

"What do you think, Emily?" Alana asked.

"Um . . . maybe," I replied.

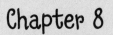

Chapter 8

The Emily Way

"Maybe? Why not yes, Emily? It's a great idea!" Natalie asked.

I didn't know what to say. Luckily, that's when my mom walked over.

"So did you come in first place?" she asked.

"Yes! We got best overall cupcakes," I told her with a big grin. I might not be sure about starting a cupcake club, but nevertheless I was still really proud of what my team and I had accomplished today!

"Well, that's wonderful!" Mom said. "Let's go out to dinner to celebrate."

Now, here's how my mom and dad are different. Not just because she has light hair and he has dark hair, like I do. But because Dad would have taken me and *all* my friends out for pizza to celebrate, while Mom took just me to a fancy restaurant. I didn't mind, actually. It got me out of having to explain why I didn't want to form our own cupcake club at Fenton!

Of course, Natalie, Alana, and Ren brought it up the next day at lunch.

"We should have our first official meeting this weekend," Natalie said.

"We could do it at my house," Ren offered. "My mom will be happy that I've already made such great friends."

"It's settled, then!" Alana declared. "What should we call ourselves? We can stick with the Mini Cupcake Club. Or maybe the Fenton Cupcake Club? Emily, do you think Katie and her friends will mind?"

"Well, I—" I began. Before I could say anything more, Ethan walked up to us.

"Hey," he said. "It's cool that your group got overall best entry yesterday. I tried one of your cupcakes. It was really good."

"Thanks," Natalie said. "I'm Natalie, our marketing agent. And this is Alana, our flavor creator, Ren, our decorator, and Emily, our baking expert."

"I'm not really an expert," I protested.

"I'm not really a flavor creator," added Alana, "Maybe more like a manager. I just want to make sure that everyone loves how our mini cupcakes taste!"

"Cool," Ethan said. "We should maybe all bake together some time. I have a great idea for a savory cupcake. It's got chicken nuggets when you bite into it, and the icing is mac and cheese!"

Ren raised her eyebrows. I tried not to make a face.

"Er, that's interesting," I said.

Ethan grinned and walked back to his table. Alana leaned forward, whispering.

"As the newly appointed manager, I think we should let him join our cupcake club," she said.

"We don't even really *have* a club yet," I reminded her. Alana looked at me funny.

Later, when I was home, I got a text on my tablet. It was from Abby.

Abby: Hey! I heard you won a cupcake contest yesterday. Congratulations!

Emily: Thanks!

I felt kind of bad. Why hadn't I let Abby know as soon as we'd won?

Actually, I knew the answer. I couldn't wait to hang out with my friends from my old school soon, but I was having so much fun with my friends from my new school that I didn't feel so lonely anymore.

Baking cupcakes with my new friends would make life at Fenton Street a lot easier, I realized. *And fun, too. But I don't want to be just like Katie!*

I had no idea what to do.

Today was a Dad day. I decided to find Katie, who was in the dining room decorating with balloons and streamers. And a handmade sign that read: EMILY IS THE BEST OVERALL!

"What's all this?" I asked.

"We're celebrating your victory at dinner tonight!" Katie cheered. "Mom has a late patient. And your dad has a meeting. But he's picking up Indian food for us."

"Mmm. Biryani?" I asked.

"Yes, your favorite. Not too spicy," Katie said. "And I made sure he asked for a double order of samosas!"

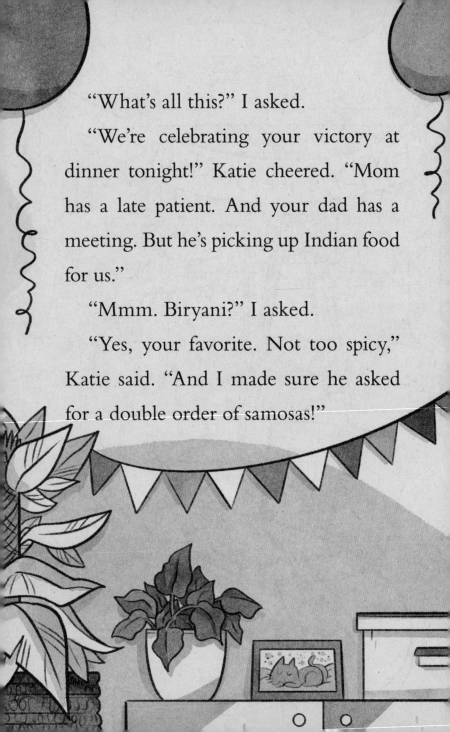

Katie is the best! I thought. Then I realized something. Being like Katie wasn't a bad thing at all. But how could I be like Katie and still be myself?

Katie noticed me frowning. "Is everything okay, Em? Not enough balloons?"

"No, the balloons are great!" I said. "It's just—my friends want us to form our own cupcake club."

"Cool!" Katie said.

"Yeah, but . . . I don't want to copy you, you know?" I said.

"I get it," Katie said. "It's like that time I thought Mom and Jeff wanted me to be more like you. I just wanted to be my own person."

"Exactly!" I said.

"But maybe this isn't the same thing," Katie went on. "You and I are different in a lot of ways. But liking to make cupcakes is one thing we have in common. So I think you should do it if you want to.

You don't have to do it my way. You can do it the Emily way. What do you think?"

The Emily way. I liked the sound of that.

"I think that could work," I said.

Katie grinned. "That's awesome, Em," she said.

"I can't wait to tell my new friends!"
I said.

We were going to form a real club! I
was going to be a member of an official
club! I didn't know what we would call
ourselves. Or what kinds of cupcakes we
would bake. But I did know some things.

We were going to do it *our* way! We weren't going to be perfect right away (or maybe ever), but it would be our own special club filled with amazing friends, lots of laughs and fun, and, of course, the most delicious cupcakes ever!

Still Hungry?

Here's a bite of the second book in the Cupcake Diaries: The New Batch series, Natalie's Double Trouble.

"Now that we're officially a club, we need to start brainstorming other events to bake for. We must keep our business going," Alana said, pushing her glasses up and pulling out her calculator.

"Ethan, your first basketball game is next Sunday, right?" I asked. Ethan nodded.

Alana looked at Ethan. "We could decorate the cupcakes for the basketball game with a basketball design!"

"That's an awesome idea," I said. *Our mini cupcakes are going to be amazing,* I thought. *We are going to be famous!*